THE SERIES

TEAM ROCKET TO THE RESCUE!

Adapted by Maria S. Barbo

Published by Scholastic Inc., *Publishers since 1920.* SCHOLASTIC and associated logos are trademarks and/or registered trademarks of Scholastic Inc.

ISBN 978-1-338-11795-0

12 11 10 9 8 7 6 5 4 3 2 1 17 18 19 20 21

Printed in the U.S.A. 40
First printing 2017

SCHOLASTIC INC.

"Best friends forever . . ." Bonnie sang to her Pokémon. "We're so happy together."

"Wow, Bonnie, what a nice song," Ash said.

"*Pika, Pika!*" Pikachu agreed.

"I call it the Squishy song!" Bonnie told her friends.

Bonnie had found Squishy— the Core Zygarde—on the way to Snowbelle City. She was on a journey with her brother, Clemont, and their friends Ash, Pikachu, and Serena.

Bonnie kissed her new Pokémon on the head. They were already best friends.

"I promise I'll never leave Squishy," she sang. "My sweet Squishy, that's you!"

Bonnie did not know that Team Rocket was watching her. They wanted to steal Squishy! As the Core Zygarde, it had amazing powers.

Jessie and James called their boss to tell him about the rare Pokémon.

"I've never seen a Pokémon like it!" James said.

"Then catch it before anyone else does," the boss said. "I'm counting on you."

“He LOVES us!” Meowth sang. Team Rocket was so happy, they felt like singing.

“And a searching we will go!” Jessie said.

“We’re outta here, yo!” Meowth howled.

They blasted off to catch Squishy.

Back by the river, Squishy was trying to nap. But something was wrong.

"Hey, Squishy," Bonnie said. "Pancham and Chespin wanna play."

Squishy was not in the mood to play. It sensed that its friend Z2 was in trouble. But Squishy was too tired to move.

"I think you're sad," Bonnie said. She tried to sing her Pokémon to sleep. She knew Squishy got its energy from the sun.

"I'll care for you and always be with you," she sang.

Squishy closed its eyes. The little Pokémon felt safe. It hoped that Z2 would be safe, too.

But Z2 was not safe. Team Flare's Weavile was chasing it through a cavern.

Druddigon blocked its path.

Z2 was trapped!

"Excellent work," said Aliana, a member of Team Flare.

Team Flare was even more dangerous than Team Rocket. They wanted to catch Z2 for their boss, too. And they had a plan.

"Z2, you're coming with us," said Mable, another Team Flare member.

But Z2 would not go without a fight.

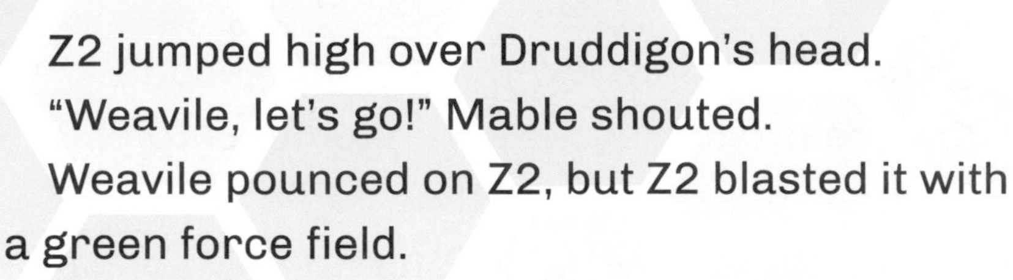

Z2 jumped high over Druddigon's head.

"Weavile, let's go!" Mable shouted.

Weavile pounced on Z2, but Z2 blasted it with a green force field.

Before Weavile could attack, Z2 sent out a call for help. Other Zygarde Core cells came from all over the canyon. They joined together to form a powerful Zygarde.

Zygarde let out a roar and charged at Druddigon's belly.

Druddigon slammed back against a cliff.

"Do it!" shouted Mable.

Team Flare aimed their blasters at Zygarde. But Zygarde was too fast. It ducked and weaved between the blasts.

"Use Dragon Pulse!" Aliana yelled.

Druddigon built up a powerful ball of energy and aimed it at Zygarde.

Rocks shattered around the Legendary Pokémon.

“Use Metal Claw!” Mable shouted.
Weavile swiped its sharp claws at Zygarde.

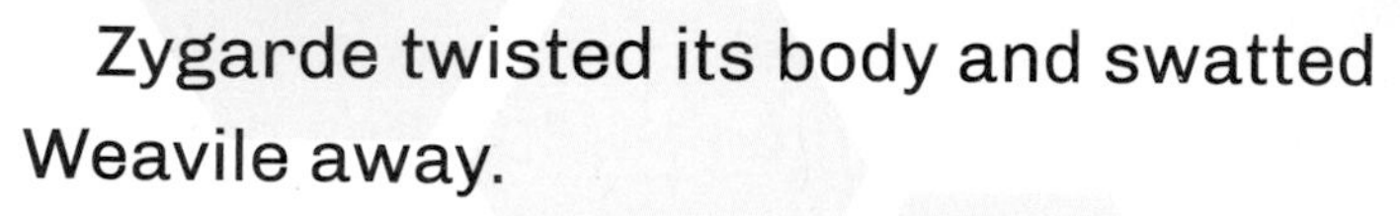

Zygarde twisted its body and swatted Weavile away.

With a mighty roar, Zygarde let loose a giant ball of energy.

The explosion sent Team Flare flying. Zygarde ran for safety.

As it ran, the Zygarde Core cells scattered. Zygarde turned back into Z2.

Z2 bounced right into the clutches of Team Rocket!

"Squishy?" Jessie asked.

"No, its markings are different," James said. "Perhaps there's more than one Squishy."

"What luck!" Jessie cried. "We've struck Squishy gold!"

"You're ours now!" Meowth purred.

But Team Flare stood in front of Team Rocket with their blasters aimed at Z2.

"It's the glasses gang!" Team Rocket shouted.

Jessie threw herself on top of Z2 to protect it. James and Meowth piled on top.

They would not let Team Flare steal their boss's new Pokémon!

"Inkay, destroy that ray!" James called. "Psybeam, touché."

Inkay's Psybeam knocked the blaster out of Mable's hand.

"All right, Gourgeist," Jessie called. "Use Seed Bomb!"

Team Flare fell to the ground in a storm of seeds.

Team Rocket fled with Z2.

"Ugh, I can't run anymore," Jessie said. They ducked behind a large rock.

"Let's take a cab next time," said Meowth.

Z2 whimpered in James's arms.

Jessie remembered spying on Squishy and Bonnie. “That twerp’s Squishy gets its energy from the sun,” she said.

“Time for some tanning,” James said. He scampered up a tall rock and placed Z2 on top.

Z2 soaked up the sun’s rays.

“Success!” James said. “You’re green with health.”

"You're not getting away this time," Aliana called.

Team Flare was back. "Playing tag is pointless and boring."

"Not on your life," James said. He cradled Z2 close to his chest.

"Dragon Pulse, go!" Aliana called.

Aliana's Druddigon blasted Team Rocket.

But James's Wobbuffet used Mirror Coat to send the pulse right back at Druddigon.

The giant Dragon-type Pokémon fell with a grunt.

"Wobbuffet rules!" Team Rocket shouted.

But the battle was not over yet.

"Use Icy Wind!" Mable called to her Weavile.

Weavile flew high into the air and blew its frozen breath right at Team Rocket. The cold gust sent them blasting off again.

"Now let's wrap this up," Aliana said.

Team Flare's Pokémon circled Z2.

But Z2 still had some moves of its own.

It sent out a call for help. Zygarde Core cells came from all over the cliffs and beyond.

Z2 grew into a bigger, more powerful Forme of Zygarde.

"That power," Aliana said. "It's the real deal!"

Zygarde roared. It unleashed a Dragon Pulse so strong it blasted a crater into the ground.

Team Flare hid behind a rock.

Zygarde reared up, ready to let loose another giant pulse.

"Oh no!" Aliana said. "Not again."

"Char!" A Charizard swooshed in and scorched Zygarde with Flamethrower.

A stranger stepped up beside Mable and Aliana. "The boss sent me to buy you some time," he told Team Flare. "Be ready."

"Now Charizard," he called. "Use Dragon Claw!"

Zygarde was too strong for Charizard. With one swat, it blasted the Fire-and-Flying-type Pokémon.

The stranger spoke into his wristband. "Respond to my heart, Key Stone!" he said. "Beyond Evolution! Mega Evolve!"

Team Flare watched as Charizard became Mega Charizard X!

"Dragon Claw!" the stranger called.

Mega Charizard X swooped into the air and attacked Zygarde with a fiery rage.

Dodge. Hit. Slam.

Mega Charizard X and Zygarde rammed into each other with equal force.

“Full power, now!” Mable ordered.

Team Flare blasted Zygarde with everything they had.

The force was too much for Zygarde. The Zygarde Core cells fled. And Zygarde turned back into Z2.

“End of the line, Z2,” Mable said.

She grabbed the Pokémon and placed it into a glowing cage.

Back in the woods, Bonnie scooped up Squishy into a big hug. She could tell when Squishy was sad.

"Everything will be okay," she told Squishy. "I'm right here with you."

Squishy and Bonnie would find Z2 and rescue it from Team Flare.

But for now, Squishy was happy to have a best friend like Bonnie to keep it safe.